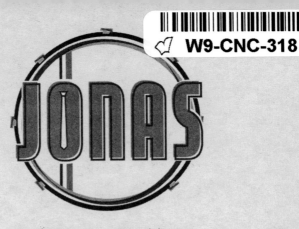

KEEPING IT REAL

Adapted by Lara Bergen

Based on the series created by Michael Curtis & Roger S. H. Schulman

Part One is based on the episode, "Keeping It Real," Written by Roger S. H. Schulman & Michael Curtis

Part Two is based on the episode, "Groovy Movies," Written by Ivan Menchell

DISNEY PRESS

New York

PART
ONE

CHAPTER ONE

It was awesome being in JONAS, the hottest rock band on the planet. As far as Kevin, Joe, and Nick Lucas could see, they had it all—fame, fans, fortune, limos, private jets . . . and, of course, girls. Well, actually, sometimes the girls could get to be a little much. But what could you expect when a band was so talented, cute, and, well . . . awesome?

Since their first album had become a huge

hit, the Lucas brothers' lives had changed a lot. Oh, they still lived at home with their mom Sandy, and dad Tom, and little brother, Frankie. And they still went to the same private high school in New Jersey, the Horace Mantis Academy. But just about everything else in their world had gotten much, much, *much* bigger.

They had moved from their old house to a really cool, huge new one. It was a renovated old firehouse, complete with fire poles and an alarm that went off randomly—not great when three teenage boys are trying to catch up on much-needed beauty sleep.

And though the three brothers still shared a room, it was practically the size of a supermarket—complete with a state-of-the-art recording studio and a row of curtained bunks, just like the ones they had installed on their tour bus. Not to mention a food court stocked with all their favorite goodies! Sometimes a little sugar went a long way. . . .

Whenever they wanted to go somewhere, they

went—to the Super Bowl or to the World Series or to Tibet to see a solar eclipse. And if they wanted to get there extrafast, they took a helicopter or a private jet. Even better? If they wanted to bring friends, it was no problem. The more, the merrier.

It didn't stop there. The oldest brother, Kevin, loved guitars. He now had not one or two or even a dozen, but *hundreds*, which he kept on a revolving dry-cleaning–style rack in their room.

All these lifestyle changes had taken some time to get used to, and some adjustments were harder than others. It had taken a little while, for example, but most of the girls at school had *finally* gotten used to having three brothers who were exceptionally cute and famous around. The guys still had to run and hide, however, whenever new girls showed up—such as the girls' chorus that had visited just the week before. They were still catching their breath from that one. And so was their bodyguard, the Big Man. Even his size, which was definitely big, couldn't intimidate some fans.

Yep, there was no doubt about it, the Lucas brothers had anything and everything in the world they could ever want (except privacy—but who cared?). They were living out their biggest dreams, and it was great. Though maybe not for everyone . . .

CHAPTER TWO

It had become a bit of a routine. As happened almost every morning, Tom Lucas, the boys' dad and manager of JONAS, was going over their schedule and other business with the boys at the breakfast table. And while she scrambled eggs and fried bacon on the stove, Sandy Lucas looked on, growing more and more irate.

"Then we do the radio interviews Saturday morning, the photo shoot in the afternoon, and the benefit concert Saturday night," Mr. Lucas read from his bulging JONAS binder. Next to him sat Nick and little Frankie. Kevin was standing nearby, headphones on and a boom mic dangling over his head.

"And the rest of the day is ours." Kevin grinned hopefully even though he knew that was highly unlikely. He turned a knob on the portable recorder strapped to his hip and adjusted his headphones slightly.

"Would anyone like some more toast?" Mrs. Lucas asked. Turning from the stove, she had to jump back suddenly as Kevin's boom mic swung around, nearly hitting her face.

"Could you say that again?" Kevin asked. "I didn't catch all of it." He held up three fingers. "In three, two, one—"

"KEVIN!" Mrs. Lucas yelled into his mic.

Kevin winced and whipped off his headphones. *Whoa!* That was really loud!

"Since when does breakfast require a microphone?" his mom asked.

6

Kevin rubbed his ear. "You know how Joe likes his pizza 'Chicago style'?" he began.

His mom nodded.

"Well, last night he took the jet to Chicago to get some."

Curly-haired Nick looked up from his plate of eggs. "He got back really late," Nick explained, "so he's sleeping in. He wanted us to record the breakfast meeting." He glanced over at Kevin. "Don't forget, he likes to hear everything, including the sizzle of the bacon."

"Thanks. Good catch," Kevin said quickly, slipping his headphones back over his ears. He swung the boom past his mom, stopping just over the frying pan.

"This is not a breakfast *meeting*," Mrs. Lucas complained, looking from Kevin, to Nick, and then to her husband. "This is *breakfast*." She put her hands on her hips and glowered at the hole in the ceiling high above their heads. "JOSEPH!" she called.

Moments later, Joe, the middle Lucas, came

sliding down the fire pole. He was still in his pajamas, his eyes were half-closed, and his normally flawless hair was a tangled mess.

"Where?! Who?! What am I missing?" he muttered as he stumbled toward the table. Yawning, he turned to Kevin. "Can you play back the tape?"

Before Kevin could hit PLAY, however, their mom pressed STOP and glared. She pointed a finger at Joe, then at the table. "Sit!"

Obediently, Joe sank into a chair. He glanced at Kevin, then Nick, as if to say, "What is up with *her*?" His brothers both shrugged back. They had no idea.

"We are having a *normal* family breakfast," Mrs. Lucas declared.

What *was* with her, was that Mrs. Lucas had had just about enough of all this big-time, jet-setting, anything-you-want-you-can-have-it lifestyle. Okay, so maybe JONAS was the biggest band in the world. But they were still a regular family. And regular families had regular meals together. And they talked to each other—she angrily swatted Kevin's boom away—*without* microphones or tape recorders.

Determined, she grabbed a plate and began to fill it with eggs and bacon and toast, just as the Big Man came strolling through the back door. Mrs. Lucas jumped—as she almost always did when she saw him. True to his name, he was a man. And he was big!

"Frankie," he announced, "I got your limo waiting."

Frankie jumped up from the table. "Is it filled with jelly beans, Big Man?" he asked.

The Big Man gave him a big thumbs-up. "Every color but green," he said, just as Frankie had asked. "It's all jelly-beany good."

Only then did Mrs. Lucas truly notice what her youngest son was wearing: a school uniform—and a fedora! She couldn't believe it. Her baby—who wasn't even *in* the JONAS band—had gone rock star on her, too. Since when did Frankie need a limo to go to school?

She watched as Frankie scooped up his backpack and followed the Big Man out the door.

Mrs. Lucas sighed and blew him a kiss. "Have fun at school, sweetie," she called. Then she set the plate she'd made for Joe down on the table. There were some things she just couldn't control.

Joe flashed her a grateful smile and began to butter his toast. His mom smiled back. Now *that*, at least, was normal. Then Joe took a bite, swallowed, and turned, frowning, to his dad. "You know, Dad, the layout in our new limo is all weird," he said.

"Really?" His dad looked up from his JONAS binder, clearly concerned. "How so?" he asked.

"Well, they put the hot tub too far away from the trampoline," Joe said.

Across the table, Nick put down his glass of juice and nodded. "And the yogurt machine makes you *choose* between chocolate and vanilla," he added. "It doesn't let you do the swirl."

Their dad shook his head, disturbed, and quickly noted this all in his book.

"Ooh!" Kevin raised his hand. "And the automatic massage seat goes 'bada-bada-bada'"— he shook his body back and forth—"when it's supposed to go 'digga-digga-digga.'"

Mr. Lucas's eyes grew steely. Now, that was bad, he thought. The massage chairs *had* to work! This would have to be fixed immediately. He reached for his phone, but his wife stopped him.

"All right, everybody, hold it!" she shouted.

Stunned, the boys and their dad paused and turned to stare at her.

"Problem, hon?" Mr. Lucas asked.

His wife rolled her eyes and shook her head. "Breakfast 'meetings,' limos with hot tubs, 'digga-digga-digga . . .' We have gotten way too big for our britches," she declared.

That's when the brothers' oldest friend and trusted style guru, Stella Malone, walked in. Stella had been in school with the boys forever and was one of the few people who didn't let their fame get to her. Today she was carrying a stack of slick-looking pants.

"Sorry I'm late," she said. "My little brother hid my car keys again." She shook her blond head then held up the pants she'd brought for them all to see. "I've got bigger britches for all of you. Custom tailored by your personal stylist, *moi*."

Stella grinned, and Mrs. Lucas groaned.

Kevin put down his mic at last and took one of the pairs of pants from Stella's arms. He held them up to his waist and smiled.

"Hey, Stella," he said suddenly, remembering something, "did you get a chance to put diamonds on the soles of my shoes?"

His mom grimaced and yanked the fancy pants away. "Stella," she said, "you're welcome to stay for breakfast, but this is exactly what I'm talking about. We said even if the band blew up, we were going to stay grounded, still be a regular family."

"Sandy, relax," said her husband. Mr. Lucas walked over and reassuringly put his arm around her shoulders. "No matter how successful this family becomes, we will *never* lose the common touch." Then with a smile, he turned and strolled to the living room, where a fancy coffee cart was parked. "Thank you, Pasquale," Mr. Lucas said to the grinning barista as the young man handed him a latte with extra foam. Mr. Lucas reached into his pocket, then tossed a coin into a tip cup.

Mrs. Lucas, meanwhile, held up her hands in desperation. Was anyone listening to her? She looked at her sons. "When was the last time anyone did chores?" she asked. "Or we had dinner together as a family?"

All at once, Nick, Joe, and Kevin each took out their phones and scrolled through their busy schedules.

"The last family dinner was three weeks ago tomorrow," Kevin said.

"And thanks for being so flexible with your schedule, Mom." Nick grinned.

Enough was enough! No more Mrs. Nice Mom, Mrs. Lucas thought. "We're a family first, and that's how we're going to start acting again," she told them. "No more breakfast meetings, limos . . ." She glanced over at Mr. Lucas. "Coffee guys!"

Kevin nodded and warmly put his arm around his mom. "We get it," he said. Everything she was saying made total sense.

Joe nodded emphatically. "We promise to keep it real."

Together, he and Kevin hugged their mother, and Nick soon jumped up and joined in. "Maybe we have gotten a little carried away," Nick said. "But that's history."

CHAPTER THREE

For the rest of the day, the boys forgot about their rock-star ways and concentrated instead on doing regular family things—such as chores.

"Mom's going to love this," Nick told Kevin as they mopped and vacuumed the floors. "A normal family, with everyone doing chores."

"Garbage bomb!" Joe called out suddenly.

Nick and Kevin looked up as six huge bags of

garbage dropped down through the fire-pole hole to the floor.

Joe soon came sliding down after them. "I cleaned under my bed!" he announced. Then he grabbed two of the bags and headed for the back door.

Seconds later, Nick and Kevin heard the shrieks of dozens of girls, followed by the *BAM!* of Joe slamming the door.

A moment later, Joe walked back into the living room. He was still holding the two trash bags, but his clothes were now completely torn to shreds. His face was pale, and he was clearly shaken.

What had they been thinking? The boys had been so busy being "normal," they'd forgotten how *not* normal some things still were—such as the fans who lurked outside waiting for them twenty-four hours a day. There was no way the brothers could ever take out the trash with all of them there, waiting to pounce.

"Keeping it real," Nick said with a sigh, "is going to be harder than we thought."

* * *

The boys weren't giving up, though. Their mom wanted a normal life back, and normal was what she was going to get. It would just have to be a different kind of normal, that was all.

They decided to wait until dark, then use the cover of night to help get the trash out. But that, unfortunately, didn't work out either. How could they have known that their fans would be armed with spotlights?

They tried every way they could think of to sneak the trash out, in fact. But nothing worked.

"We need a new plan," Nick said finally. "Which plan are we up to?"

Kevin flipped open a memo pad. "Plan K," he read.

"Right," said Nick. "This is going to require some thought." He looked from Joe to Kevin. "Ready?" he said. "Go." It was JONAS thinking time!

Five minutes passed. Then ten. JONAS thinking time was taking *too* much time. "I've got it," Nick said finally, after an hour or so. He had a Plan K. All they needed were some tools: calipers, heavy-duty pulleys, and lots and lots of rope.

Once those things were found (a surprisingly easy chore), Nick and Kevin got busy nailing a pulley to their window.

"Dude, this window frame is rock solid," Kevin said, knocking on the wood.

"One of the advantages of living in an old firehouse," Nick replied.

Kevin grinned. "I *wondered* why there were fire poles here!" he cried.

Good old Kevin, Nick thought, stifling a smile. He went back to hammering. Kevin didn't always catch on quickly but it was just part of his charm.

Just then, Joe walked up in a jumpsuit, a harness, and night-vision goggles. The two bags of garbage were gripped tightly in his hands.

Joe took a deep breath and squared his shoulders as Kevin hooked him up to the rope.

"Your code name is Danger," Kevin reminded him. That shouldn't be too hard to remember—it was what Joe liked to call himself—plan or no plan. Kevin patted Joe's shoulder, then tested the clip. "After we lower you down," he went on, "we'll be in constant contact." Then he turned to a nearby amp and microphone and switched them on.

"Just get in and get out," Nick instructed. "We don't need any heroes."

Joe narrowed his eyes like a man on a mission—which he sort of was. "It's time to take out the trash," he said with a confident nod.

Then Kevin and Nick hoisted him over the windowsill and began, ever so carefully, to lower him down. They could hear Joe's voice, loud and clear, through the amplifier in their room: "This is Danger. No girls in sight. Heading to the garbage cans."

"I think he's going to make it," Nick said, daring to smile.

Kevin nodded and went to trade a high five. Then, the static began.

"I think I saw something," Joe whispered. His voice was tense . . . and afraid. "Shadows . . . Wait . . ."

Then suddenly, the sound of girls screaming filled the air: "AAAAHHH! JOE! I LOVE YOU!!!!"

"It's an ambush!" Joe cried. "I can't—too many—the perfume—ahhh!"

Then only silence.

"Danger's in danger!" Kevin cried.

Nick, meanwhile, lunged for the rope. "Get him out of there!" he hollered.

They hauled up the rope as fast as they could. But when the tattered line came up, there was trash on it—but no Joe.

CHAPTER FOUR

The next morning, the boys went to school utterly exhausted.

"Four hours taking out the garbage and all night rehearsing," Nick moaned as he worked to open his locker. "I am wiped."

"You mean *trying* to take out the garbage," Joe corrected. He shuddered as he recalled the terrifying moments from the night before. He had managed to escape—barely. "We never got rid of the stuff. Where'd you put it, Kev?" he asked. He turned to his older brother, who was leaning against the locker on his other side. Kevin was wearing a pair of dark sunglasses and a particularly solemn expression.

"Kev?" Joe asked again. He poked his brother's shoulder, and with a jerk, Kevin straightened up.

"George Washington!" he cried, whipping off his sunglasses and quickly raising his hand. Then he paused and looked around. "That was just a dream?" he asked. His brothers nodded, and he sighed. "Good," he said, relieved, "because I was dreaming I was in math class."

Stella, meanwhile, was walking down another hall of Horace Mantis with her good friend, Macy Misa. Unlike Stella, Macy was far from feeling comfortable around her idols, the JONAS band. She couldn't help it; she adored them and tended to faint whenever they were around. As the president of their fan club, this was a slightly inconvenient habit.

"So if I can get an exclusive interview with

Kevin for my JONAS Web site," she was telling Stella, "the entire fan club will be *blown* away." Her face lit up at the thought.

"So interview him," Stella told her matter-of-factly.

"I don't know . . ." Macy shook her head. Maybe for Stella that was easy. But for her? Not so much. "Sometimes I get a teensy bit nervous when I get a teensy bit near a JONAS," she said.

Stella tried not to smile too much. *That* was an understatement. But Macy had no reason to be afraid of the band. After all, Stella had known the boys forever. Beneath all their fame and fortune—and supercute looks—they were just like everyone else. She hoped that someday her friend would see past all that and down to who the brothers really were.

"Hey, look," said Stella suddenly as they turned a corner. "There's Kevin." This was as a good a time as any to start.

Macy's eyes grew wide—then rolled back in her head.

Stella tried to keep her from falling. "I've got your back," she said. She shook Macy a few times by the shoulders to snap her out of it, then she grabbed the girl by the arms and dragged her to the wall where Kevin was leaning. He had put his sunglasses back on, and neither Stella nor Macy had any idea that he was, once again, fast asleep.

"Kevin," Stella began, "you know my BFF, Macy. She'd like to ask you a question for her JONAS–fan-club blog thing." She nudged Macy forward with an encouraging wink. "Go!"

Macy swallowed once. Then twice. Then two more times. It felt as if her mouth, her throat, her chest . . . her whole body was going to explode!

"Uh, Kevin of JONAS," she finally blurted, "our entire fan club wants to know, who's your favorite JONAS?" As soon as the words were out of her mouth, she wished she could take them back. It *was* a ridiculous question to ask one of the band members. Still, what was done was done. She stood, her whole body trembling, waiting breathlessly for his reply.

Kevin, of course, didn't move.

Macy, at last, held up her notebook. "'No comment at this time,'" she noted, nodding. Then she turned to Stella with a dreamy, adoring smile. "The brilliant diplomat, as always," she said.

"Thanks, Kev," Stella said brightly, waving to him with a grateful smile. "You're a great interview."

Then she helped a blissful Macy move away—just before Kevin began to snore.

CHAPTER FIVE

After getting home from school that afternoon, the brothers tried, once again, to tackle their "normal" chores, this time cleaning their room. But before they knew it, all three of them were asleep on their feet—literally.

"Boys!" their mother called from the living room below.

Nick was the first to wake up. "Mom's coming!" he warned the others. "Look alive!" He grabbed the vacuum he'd been sleeping on and began to push it across the floor.

"I can't," groaned Joe. He yawned and pulled away from the recording-booth window, where he had been dusting and then sleeping—leaving a long line of drool behind him. He raised his rag and wearily wiped it away.

"Then at least keep your eyes open," Nick told him. "If Mom thinks we can't handle simple chores, she'll be really bummed."

Joe knew Nick was right, and he tried his best to rally as his mom and dad walked in.

"What are you guys up to?" Mr. Lucas asked.

"Just cleaning," Nick said. He grinned and pointed to Joe, then Kevin, who, he just then realized, was *still* asleep. He grabbed a rag and threw it at him, causing Kevin to wake up . . . and slide down the fire pole which had been propping him up.

"Whoa!" Kevin cried as he fell. Then from below, he called out cheerfully, "Pole's clean!"

"You guys okay?" their mom asked.

"Fine," Nick assured her. He gripped the handle of the vacuum and began pushing it industriously.

Joe covered a yawn with his cleaning rag. "Sure," he agreed.

Then Kevin ran up the stairs to join them. "We're cool. Why do you ask?" he said.

"Well, first off," said his dad, "Nick's vacuum isn't turned on."

Nick looked down at the silent appliance in his hand, then across to the cord. He made a face. It wasn't even plugged in! "I'm rehearsing vacuuming," he said quickly.

Their mom just smiled. "It means so much to me to see you guys making such an effort to be a normal family," she told them.

Nick nodded heartily. "We are *so* all over the normal," he said.

"And tonight's our family dinner," Mrs. Lucas went on, rubbing her hands. "I'm making my special fried chicken."

"With the homemade bread crumbs!" added their dad.

Mmm! They could taste the goodness already! A real home-cooked meal—not something fancy and gourmet made by a personal chef. How long had it been?

"How do you make bread crumbs, anyway?" Kevin asked.

Mr. Lucas thought for a minute. "It's complicated," he frowned. "You have to take the bread . . ." He rubbed his chin. "Then you have to crumb it."

His wife rolled her eyes good-naturedly. "Close enough, dear," she said. They were still a long way from completely normal. But the important thing was they were making progress, and she didn't want to stop now. "Listen, boys," she went on, "there are some bags of your old clothes downstairs. Would you mind dropping them off at the thrift store?"

Nick instantly grinned and parked his vacuum. He was all about getting out of cleaning. "We'll drop the stuff off now and be back in time for the family dinner," he told her.

His brothers nodded in agreement, and Mrs. Lucas smiled at each of them warmly. "I'm so proud of you guys," she said.

Their dad gave them two thumbs-up. And then he and his wife left the room, arm in arm.

Once they were gone, Joe's face fell. "How are we going to sneak out of here without getting mobbed by fans?" he asked the others. Maybe his brothers had already forgotten about last night's garbage debacle. But he sure hadn't! The screaming . . . the tearing . . . It was enough to give a guy nightmares for life.

"Don't worry," Kevin said. "I know how to give us a head start." He grabbed the scarf from around Joe's neck. Then he threw open the window. Instantly, the sound of screaming girls filled the air.

"Who wants a scarf?" Kevin hollered. Then he tossed out the piece of fabric, letting the breeze take it away. He waited for the screams to double, then he closed the window again.

"Hey, that was my favorite scarf," Joe

complained. Granted, he had about eight hundred others. But still . . .

Nick, however, got the bigger picture. "Awesome!" he told Kevin. "While they're tearing apart Joe's favorite scarf, we can sneak out the back way!"

Kevin looked surprised. He hadn't gotten that far exactly. "Hey, *that's* a great idea, too."

CHAPTER SIX

A short while later, the boys arrived safely at a store downtown that specialized in cool vintage clothing. They were cautious but pleased. Between their scarf trick and the hooded sweatshirts, sunglasses, and caps they had put on, they had accomplished the impossible: escaping their fans!

The store was empty, so Nick hit the bell on the counter a few times. They waited, and in a few seconds, Macy Misa stepped out from the back.

"May I help—*AHHHHHHHHHH!*" she screamed, recognizing all three of them instantly, despite their get-ups.

The boys dove for cover, then slowly emerged one by one when they thought it was safe.

"I think she's going to explode," Nick observed.

Indeed, Macy was frozen in a position that looked combustible. Her eyes were wide and her mouth was stretched into a clownlike grin, while her arms stuck out straight from her sides as if she were frozen in midhug. And it seemed as if she wasn't breathing since she was beginning to turn blue. . . .

They had to do something. "Take some deep breaths," Joe said encouragingly. He demonstrated for Macy—inhaling and exhaling.

"In with the good air, out with the weird air," Kevin said, joining in.

Macy shuddered as she pulled in one wheezing breath.

"Better?" Nick asked gently.

Macy let out the air and nodded very slowly. However, she was still incapable of moving the rest of her body—including her mouth. The sight of JONAS in the store had rendered her speechless *and* immobile. When it became obvious that Macy wasn't going to start talking, Joe took action.

"So, you work here after school?" he casually asked her.

Macy gulped. Was he really . . . *talking* to her? As though they were *friends*? This had to be a dream. She pinched herself.

Ouch! Okay, not a dream. "My mom owns the store, Joe of JONAS," she finally managed to answer. "Sometimes I watch it for her. Like today." She bit her lip and sniffed as a tear of joy welled in her eye. "The greatest day of my life," she added.

The Lucas brothers exchanged looks. Suddenly, they *really* missed normal. *A lot.*

Normal or not, they had to keep moving. The

scarf trick wasn't going to last forever. "Uh . . . okay," Joe said. Then he nodded at the bags they'd brought in. "We want to drop off some clothes—" But he didn't get to finish his sentence.

"Omigosh!" exclaimed Macy. "Actual clothes worn by the actual JONAS band. Brought in by actual *JONASes*." The idea was too . . . too everything! She paused to pinch herself—again. Ouch! That *really* hurt! But she didn't care. "This is actually happening!" she cried.

Just then, a girl who looked about eleven walked into the store. She was dressed head to toe in JONAS gear, including a #1 JONAS FAN! T-shirt. She took one look at the boys in front of her and, well, naturally, screamed.

The brothers winced as the girl kept screaming and began to fumble around in her backpack. In an instant her hand came out holding something small.

Joe was the first to ID it. "Camera phone!"

All three knew what to do. They tried to hit

the deck, but there was a click before they could move.

Nick turned to his brothers. This was not good. "If she sends that picture, we're going to be surrounded by screaming—"

There was no need for Nick to finish his sentence. Joe and Kevin knew all too well what would happen if their "#1 fan" sent the text she was typing. In desperation, they reached out, hoping to stop her. But they were a second too slow. She pressed SEND.

"NOOOOOOO!" Joe howled. Fearfully, he turned toward the store window. It was too late. They were surrounded already.

There was no way they were getting out of the vintage store anytime soon. They were well and truly stuck.

"Something tells me that Mom's going to be having that normal family dinner without us," Joe said sadly.

"At least all this screaming will drown out the sound of Mom's heart breaking," Nick said, trying, as always, to look on the bright side.

Kevin put his hand to his ear. "Nope. I heard it," he said. It was too loud to miss.

CHAPTER SEVEN

It wasn't as if the JONAS band had never been surrounded before. They had had their fair share of unwanted run-ins with fans, photographers, and hovering helicopters. But this was a new situation. They had never gotten trapped when they'd promised their mom that they'd be home for dinner *no matter what*.

Kevin peered out the store's window and let out a moan. "We're trapped like rats!" he said miserably. "Filthy, disgusting, rock-and-roll rats."

"There has to be another way out of here," Nick said, looking around. He turned eagerly to Joe, who'd gone off in search of a back door and was just returning.

"The back way's no good," Joe informed his brothers with a sigh.

"Why not?" Kevin asked.

"There *is* no back way," Joe explained. There was just a crowded old storeroom. No door. No window. Nothing.

Nick ran his hands through his curly brown hair. "I can't believe this," he said. "All we were trying to do is help our mom!"

"This is all *your* fault!" Macy said, turning on the text-happy "#1 fan." She pointed to the girl's T-shirt. For a moment, the boys thought Macy was going to come to their rescue. But then she continued, "'Number-one JONAS fan!'? I don't *think* so, princess!" She ripped open her own button-down shirt to reveal a T-shirt underneath.

It read #1 SUPER JONAS FAN! Macy raised her chin and coolly glared.

But the other girl was not about to be intimidated. She put her hands on her hips and narrowed her eyes. "Your powers are no match for mine!" she declared.

The three boys exchanged looks. Had they entered an alternate dimension?

Apparently so.

A millisecond later, Macy was grabbing the "enemy" by the collar and pants and tossing her out of the store.

At the sight of the open door, of course, the rest of the fans clamoring outside ran up and tried to push their way in. The force was as unstoppable—and powerful—as a tidal wave. It was all Macy and the boys could do to get the door closed again.

One tall, blond girl, however, seemed even more determined than the rest. "Let. Me. In!" she yelled above the screams of the maddening crowd. It took a minute for the guys to realize it wasn't some crazed fan at all . . . it was Stella.

Joe reached out and quickly pulled her in. Then, using all their combined strength, they firmly slammed the door.

"So . . ." Stella said, after taking a minute to catch her breath, "I got your nine-one-one." She gazed around the store. "What's up?" To her, it looked like just another day out for the world-famous JONAS.

Joe shrugged. "Oh, nothing. Just wanted to hang."

"Thought you'd like to join us," added Nick.

"Plus"—Kevin spoke up—"we'll never make Mom's dinner, we're going to destroy our family, and our lives are over!"

Calmly, Stella reached into her bag and took out her phone. "No problem," she told them. "Let's just call your parents and tell them what's going on."

"No!" Joe grabbed Stella's hand to keep her from using the phone. "Mom already thinks it's impossible for us to be a normal family."

"We couldn't even take out the trash," Kevin explained.

"Then let's call the police," Stella suggested. That seemed like a logical solution.

But Nick frowned. "We can't call the police every time we have to run an errand for Mom," he argued. "How is that 'keeping it real'?"

"Besides," Macy spoke up, "the police won't come here anymore. Not since my Aunt Martha called them thirty-six times in one day. She thought the mannequin kept 'looking' at her." Macy took in the group's rather disconcerted faces. "Yeah . . ." She nodded. "She's a kook."

Nick cut a quick glance to the mannequin, just to be sure it wasn't "looking" at him, too. When he was sure they weren't being watched, he turned back. In quiet desperation he gazed around the rest of the store. "Then I guess we live here now," he muttered.

Macy's face lit up immediately. That sounded fine by her. "Problem solved!" she cried. Talk about getting an inside scoop for the fan club!

Of course, she realized it really wasn't a great solution. Still . . .

Joe wasn't ready to give up the fight quite yet. He jumped up on an old wooden crate. On its side was the word SOAP.

"Wait a minute!" he said. "What's happened to our JONAS spirit?" He looked down at his brothers, determined. "Remember when we tried to take out the garbage?" he asked them. "Kevin, you were all, 'Let's take out the garbage!' And Nick, you were like, 'Look at us, all takin' out the garbage!' And I was 'Wooo! I'm Joe, and I'm takin' out the garbage! Wooo!'"

Nick and Kevin stared back at him, equally uninspired.

"Joe," Nick reminded him, "we never actually got the garbage out."

"But we didn't get it out with *teamwork*!" Joe declared. He and his brothers worked best together. They couldn't forget that.

Slowly, Kevin nodded. Maybe, just maybe, Joe had something there. "We just need to come up with a plan," Kevin said. He gazed around at the girls and his brothers. "Everybody think," he said seriously.

And so they did . . .

CHAPTER EIGHT

"I can't take it anymore!" Joe cried a short while later. He was pacing the floor. Thinking, it seemed, had only made things *much* worse. Now Joe felt trapped in the store—like a captive in some late-night made-for-TV movie. "The walls! The walls are closing in!" he cried. He clutched his stomach suddenly. "What if we run out of food?!"

"Oh, don't worry about food," Macy assured

him. She pulled a well-worn leather handbag down off a shelf near the front of the store. "Inside some of these old purses, you can find mints." She opened it up and, sure enough, pulled a half-empty pack out.

"Okay," Joe said, feeling just a little calmer. Then the panic hit him again. "What if we run out of water?!" he choked. He felt his throat closing up—he was sure it was only a matter of moments. All the fame, the fun . . . gone. "Water! I need water!"

"Calm down, dude," said Nick. He took a swig from a big bottle of water he'd had with him the whole time. Then he handed it to his brother. "Here."

Joe grabbed it and gulped down the clear liquid. "Ahhhh," he sighed. He grinned. "Now with a hint of lime!"

Macy, meanwhile, popped a stale mint into her mouth, then sidled timidly over to Kevin. "Kevin of JONAS?" she said slowly.

"Hey, Macy," he said.

She took a deep breath and tried not to squeal. He had said her name!

"Now that we're all trapped here in my mom's store, probably for all eternity, which is a real bummer for you but a dream come true for me"—Macy paused to smile dreamily—"maybe you could answer some more questions for my fan site?"

Kevin watched, wide-eyed, as Macy held up a huge stack of index cards. It looked like she had enough questions to fill the entire Web. "Uh . . . sure." He shrugged.

Macy bit her lip and pinched herself. *Ouch!*

"Okay, first question," she said. "'Would you ever kiss a girl on the first date?'" She stopped and read the question one more time to herself. "Date a JONAS . . . Kiss a JONAS . . ." she murmured, growing pale. The whole idea was *way* too much for her to handle. Before Kevin could even answer, Macy fainted.

Kevin shook his head. Poor Macy, he thought.

He looked down at her, glad that she'd at least landed on the rug. Then he reached down and picked up one of the hundreds of cards that she had dropped.

"'What is your favorite animal?'" he read. He thought about it for a moment. This was a tough one. "I'd have to go with a bear in a bikini," he finally said with a grin. Then he pulled Macy's pen from her limp hand and jotted his answer down on the card.

Stella, meanwhile, was still trying to think. "There has to be *some* way we can get you out of here," she told the band. "Why do you guys have to have the most recognizable faces in the world?" she complained.

"Really?" said Kevin, turning to the closest mirror. "I have a recognizable face?"

Nick nodded. "I'd recognize it anywhere," he said.

Suddenly Joe smiled and looked over at his brothers. He finally had an idea! "I'll wear a disguise!" he cried. Grabbing a bow tie off a shelf, he put it around his neck. "See?" he said, feeling clever and completely unrecognizable—which was clearly *not* the case. "It's still me—Joe!"

Kevin and Nick rolled their eyes. But Stella's blue ones lit up.

"Joe, you're a genius!" she exclaimed. She motioned to the racks and racks of vintage clothes around them. "We're surrounded by costumes," she went on. "I bet I can disguise you guys enough to sneak through the fans." After all, she *was* a fabulous designer. This would just be like a test.

"Excellent!" Kevin exclaimed. "I'll go disguised as Joe. Joe can go as Nick. And Nick can go as me." He looked eagerly at Stella, who tried her best not to groan.

"You know," she told Kevin, "that idea is *so* good, we should save it for the next time we're stuck somewhere." Then she headed for the racks and began to pull out *real* costumes.

The boys tried on almost everything that Stella

could find in the store: Clark Kent glasses and a suit; a baseball uniform; a turn-of-the-century explorer's costume; a sailor suit; cowboy clothes; a mechanic's outfit; caveman wear; a Santa Claus costume . . . and a Santa Claus costume again. But nothing was quite right. Still, Stella refused to give up. Finally, she handed the boys three sets of doctor's scrubs—complete with surgical masks—and waited one more time for them to emerge from the dressing room.

When they came out, Stella stepped back and surveyed her work, rather pleased. "What do you think, guys?" she asked.

"Comfortable," Nick said.

Kevin nodded and swung his arms back and forth. "Roomy."

"I look great!" Joe declared. He stood, admiring himself from all sides in the nearby full-length mirror. "I should go to medical school," he said.

Just then, Joe's cell phone rang. He looked down to check the caller ID and winced. "It's Dad!" he cried.

"Don't tell him what's going on!" Nick warned sternly. They were close to escape and couldn't risk anything going wrong now.

Joe nodded as he nervously answered the phone. "Hello, Father," he said, trying his best to sound extracalm. "Yes, as Mother requested, we're at the thrift store." He paused to listen to his father's next question. "We're running a little late because"—he made a face—"we found a stray . . ."

"Puppy! Kitten! Umbrella!" Stella, Nick, and Kevin all cried out at once.

"Bunny," Joe blurted out instead. "But don't worry," he added quickly. "We found it a good home. See you soon!" He flipped the phone closed as fast as he could. "We hope."

"Okay," Nick said, clapping his hands. There was no time to lose. "Get into character," he told the others. "We're three doctors who just got beeped with a dire emergency."

Kevin frowned. He didn't want to just be any old doctor. "*I'm* a successful brain surgeon," he clarified.

Nick rolled his eyes. "Whatever." Then he glanced down at Macy, still lying passed out on the floor. He guessed they'd have to leave her there . . . or was she just what they needed to *really* make their disguises work?!

He nodded to Joe and then toward Macy, and together they knelt down beside her. Nick grabbed her shoulders and Joe took her ankles. Carefully, they lifted her up.

"Poor thing," said Stella. "If she only knew she was being carried by two-thirds of JONAS, she'd faint." She shook her head sadly, then moved to the front door, opening it gingerly, wary of the flood of fans.

"Out of the way, please," Kevin announced in his most serious, successful, brain-surgeon-sounding voice. "Overwhelmed fan coming through."

The mob just kept yelling and screaming, too obsessed with JONAS-spotting to move.

Kevin cleared his throat. Then he hollered, "She just puked!"

Instantly, the crowd cleared a wide path for them.

It looked as if they were good to go, and then Nick's phone rang. He dropped Macy's feet to answer it. "Hi, Mom," he said.

The crowd leaned forward a little bit to hear.

"No, everything's totally normal. You'd be proud of how normal we are," Nick went on. "Why do you ask?"

"Oh, just curious," his mom answered, "because it looks like you're in a little trouble."

Nick's mouth fell open. What? he thought. How could his mom possibly know that they were in trouble? And how, he also wondered, could she sound so *close*—almost as if she weren't even on the phone? That's when Kevin tapped him on the shoulder. Nick turned. There were his mom *and* his dad *and* his little brother.

The boys were so stunned, they completely forgot about the enthusiastic fans surrounding them. One by one, they pulled down their doctors' masks, ready to come clean to their mom. As soon as the fans recognized them as JONAS, they started to scream. There was no other choice. . . .

"RETREAT!!" Nick cried.

CHAPTER NINE

It wasn't easy, but at last, Nick, Joe, and Kevin, their brother and parents, and Stella and Macy (who was finally awake) safely made it back into the vintage store.

Then Mrs. Lucas turned to the boys, her arms crossed. "What is going on here?" she asked.

Nick forced a grin. "We're three doctors who just got beeped with a dire emergency," he told her.

"*I'm* a successful brain surgeon," Kevin clarified.

Their mom looked at them sternly. Those weren't the answers she was looking for. They knew it and shuffled their feet and sighed.

"We were dropping the clothes off, and we got surrounded by fans," Joe finally confessed.

"Why didn't you call?" Mrs. Lucas asked. "We would have gotten you out of this." Her stern expression instantly changed into a concerned one.

"Because we know how important it is for you that we keep it real," Joe replied.

"Awww . . ." His mom's face softened into a smile, and her eyes began to well with tears. All this trouble . . . all this craziness and costumes . . . was for her? She was touched.

Kevin hated to see his mom cry, even if her tears were happy ones. He reached out and wrapped his arms around her. "Family hug," he declared. And soon everyone joined in. Outside, girls screamed, but inside the store, things felt truly . . . normal.

Pulling away, Mr. Lucas reached down to pick up a large picnic basket that he had carried in. "Now can we eat?" he asked, a twinkle in his eye.

"What do you mean, 'eat'?" Nick asked.

Mrs. Lucas wiped her last tear away. "I am determined that we're going to have at least one meal together as a family," she said, looking each boy in the eye. Then she smiled. "No reason a family dinner can't be a picnic."

Joe's eyes grew wide. He wasn't going to starve! Or have to eat clothing . . . or worse. They were saved! "You have *food*? I love you, Mom!" he cried. Then he lunged for the basket and tore it open. Instantly, the smell of their mom's fried chicken filled the air. Joe grabbed the first chicken leg he could find and took a ravenous bite. "This is the most fantastic fried chicken you've ever made!" he exclaimed.

Beaming, she passed out plates and napkins and containers of food to everyone. "And don't worry, guys," she said as they all began to dig in, "the Big Man's outside. He'll get us out of this."

Just then, the Big Man walked through the door, his clothes ripped to shreds. He looked shaken . . . and scared.

"There were little girls everywhere. It was a nightmare," he said, his deep voice trembling. "But don't worry," he assured the boys, "I'm not leaving your side." Then he spotted a rack in the corner. "Ooh! Funny hats!" he exclaimed, trotting across the room.

Mrs. Lucas gazed from the Big *Distracted* Man to the mob lurking outside, which only seemed to have grown. "You think there's enough room in the parking lot to land the JONAS jet?" she wondered. How else could they get out of here?

"That's not exactly keeping it real, Mom," Nick pointed out.

Mrs. Lucas sighed. "I guess I'm just going to have to get used to the fact that my kids are superstars, and sometimes superstars can't keep it real."

Kevin wrapped his arms around her once more. No question, his mom was the best! "Okay," he said, "another family hug!" He really was a softie when it came to hugs.

They made a happy huddle again. When they pulled back, however, they discovered it wasn't exactly a family huddle. They'd included Macy.

"Sorry, didn't see you there," Joe said.

"No problem," Macy told him. Then, of course, she fainted.

But the Lucas family still had bigger problems: like how to get out of the shop—alive.

"Wait a minute," Mr. Lucas said suddenly. "We still have one weapon in our arsenal." He pulled a bowl out of the picnic basket. "Mom's amazing potato salad!"

The boys couldn't believe it, but it worked: their mom's potato salad provided just enough crowd control to get them out of the thrift shop and into their limo.

As they pulled away, Mr. Lucas warmly squeezed his wife's shoulder. "You got your family dinner, hon."

Mrs. Lucas nodded. "With three hundred of our closest friends."

PART ONE

Stella Malone points out to her friend Macy Misa that the members of JONAS are coming their way.

Joe and Nick Lucas give their brother Kevin a wake-up call when they find him sleeping against his locker.

Joe is prepared for anything—even a stampede of
screaming girls!

Kevin demonstrates some of his signature
rock-star moves.

Uh-oh! Fans have trapped the boys inside a
clothing store!

The brothers have to sneak out of the store without
being noticed. It's time for a costume change.

Nick peeks out from the dressing room, wearing his idea of a good getaway outfit.

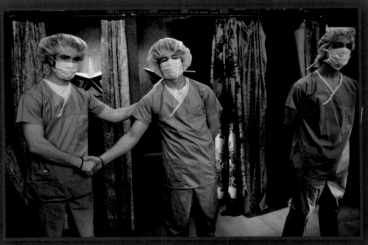

Paging Dr. JONAS. The boys have found the perfect disguises!

PART TWO

Oh, no! Kevin, Nick, and Joe don't know what their mom wants for her birthday!

"Your dad found the old home movies I thought we lost in the move," Mrs. Lucas tells her sons.

Watching their old home movies, the brothers know exactly what to give their mother for her birthday.

"Gentleman, let's bake a cake!" Nick declares.

"Dudes, that's not a bowl—that's a colander!" Nick cries. All the batter has seeped out of the bowl— and destroyed their mom's videos.

Nick and Kevin dress up in their old Halloween costumes—a cowboy and Abe Lincoln!

"We all know what's going to happen. I drink the eggnog, my headgear makes it spill down the front of me, and I get a rash on Christmas," Stella protests.

The family watches their new home movies. Kevin, Joe, and Nick's hard work has paid off—their mom loves her birthday present!

CHAPTER TEN

The next day, Nick and Joe looked up from their sports sections and guitar magazines to see Kevin march into the living room covered in trash—or covered in big *bags* of trash, to be exact. They were attached to his body, like a giant trash suit.

"Kev, where are you going?" Nick asked.

"Out," Kevin replied, his face hard with determination.

"Like *that*?" Joe asked. "This is meant with love, but . . . you look a little *trashy*." He grinned at his pun and winked at Nick.

"Maybe you can admit failure," Kevin told him. "Let others say you were beaten by garbage. But not me. This chore will not defeat me!" And with that, he walked up to his brothers and clasped them on the shoulders.

Nick and Joe both tried to hold their breath. The suit was a little—make that a lot—stinky.

"Good-bye," Kevin said. Then he walked over to the front door and grabbed the knob.

"Don't do it!" Nick called after him. "It isn't worth it!"

"You're throwing your life away, man!" Joe told him.

But Kevin opened the door anyway, and with a battle cry—"*YAAAAAAAAAAA!*"—he charged out.

The next thing the brothers heard was the sound of girls screaming. Then something that sounded a lot like wild animals ripping and tearing something apart.

Then silence.

Joe turned to Nick. "That doesn't sound good," he said.

Anxiously, they waited for a sign of life. Finally, the door slowly opened, and Kevin returned . . . as good as new.

Nick and Joe couldn't believe it. The girls had torn off every bit of trash that Kevin had attached to himself but had left his clothes intact. Beaming, Kevin held up his hands, and his brothers congratulated him with high fives. Mission accomplished!

Who said superstars couldn't take out the trash?

PART
TWO

CHAPTER ONE

For the world-famous JONAS band, it was just another day at school. The youngest band member, Nick Lucas, was pulling books out of his locker when his older brother Kevin walked up and slapped him on the arm.

"Hey, what are you giving Mom and Dad for their anniversary tomorrow?" he asked casually.

Nick spun around, slack-jawed. "Tomorrow's their anniversary?!" he exclaimed. "Nobody told me!" He started to panic right away. "I don't have time to get them anything! I'm in school all day, and then we rehearse all night!" He quickly tried to come up with some kind of solution to this massive problem. Then he stopped. "Wait a minute," he said to Kevin. "Their anniversary's not for, like, months."

Kevin couldn't help laughing. "Psych!" he crowed.

Nick grimly slammed his locker shut and glared at him. "Not cool."

"Dude, you are *soooo* easy," Kevin said, still chuckling.

"What's so funny?" Joe, the middle brother, asked, walking up to join them.

Still laughing, Kevin pointed at Nick and recounted the episode. "I go, 'Hey, Nick, what are you giving Mom and Dad for their anniversary?' And then, he's all, 'Oh, no, I forgot. I don't have time to get them anything!' And I go, 'Psych!' And he goes, 'Not cool.' And then you walk up and ask, 'What's so funny?' And then I go 'Hey,

Nick.'" Kevin paused to catch his breath.

Joe held up his hand. "I'm caught up," he said, stopping Kevin before he launched into the story again—and again. Then he turned to Nick. "I can't believe you still fall for that," he scolded. "Especially when it's not their anniversary . . . it's Dad's *birthday*." He looked at his brothers expectantly. But they only shook their heads and grinned. "What?" Joe said earnestly. "I'm not playing."

"I'm not going for that twice," Nick said, shooting his brother a stern look.

Joe shrugged and opened up his own locker and pulled out an enormous card. "Check out this crazy big card I got him," he told Nick and Kevin. On the outside it read HAPPY BIRTHDAY, DAD in giant letters.

Instantly, Nick and Kevin paled. Joe wasn't fooling around.

"Oh, man," Kevin cried. "I can't believe I forgot Dad's birthday."

"I forgot last year, too!" Nick moaned.

Joe nodded with satisfaction, then opened up the card. Inside, in even larger letters, it read PSYCH!

Nick and Kevin began to fume.

Joe laughed. "I am *awesome!*"

Before Nick and Kevin could do physical harm to their brother, their friend Stella Malone walked up and joined them. "Hey, you guys think your mom will like this for her birthday?" she asked. She pulled a hideous-looking sweater out of a shopping bag and held it up.

Joe, Kevin, and Nick looked at each other. Stella Malone was the most fashionable girl, by far, in school. She was so good, they'd even made her their band's stylist. She was the first to pop a new-style fedora on her blond head or match skinny jeans with an oversize belt. No way would she pick something like that out for anyone—let alone their *mother.* Did she *really* think they would fall for a trick like that? They weren't born yesterday, after all. *Please!*

"Nice attempt, Stella," said Kevin, "but I just

pulled the same scam two minutes ago."

"And I just pulled it two seconds ago," said Joe.

"And I am not falling for it a third time!" Nick declared.

"Besides," Joe went on, "that's the ugliest thing I've ever seen. You would never give that to our mom." He shared a look with his brothers. Nice try, Stella Malone, they all seemed to be thinking.

"Okay." Stella sighed. "You win. I would *never* give her this. What I *really* got her is this André Foulard silk scarf from Paris." And with that, she pulled a truly beautiful, long, silk scarf out of her bag.

"Now *that's* something she would give to our mom," Nick said.

Joe and Kevin looked at him—and then back at the ultrachic scarf.

"You guys forgot her birthday, didn't you?" Stella said, her expression a cross between shock and disappointment.

"No."

"No way."

"Of course not."

Nick, Joe, and Kevin all shook their heads emphatically. Then they spun around and took off, running down the hallway.

Stella neatly folded the scarf and returned it to her bag as she watched them go. They had *totally* forgotten. Typical! she thought.

"I think the school store is still open!" Stella cried to their retreating backs. Maybe they would find something decent inside. Maybe.

CHAPTER TWO

Unfortunately for the Lucas brothers, the school store turned out to be out of almost everything but protractors—and after her last birthday, their mom had plenty of those.

"I have no idea what to get Mom," Nick groaned as they sat around their bedroom loft, sulking, after school.

Joe was trying to do his homework, and Kevin was trying to tune a few guitars, but Nick was determined to figure out *something* to do for their mom. He sat on his bed with a pile of women's magazines in front of him, hoping to find inspiration.

"Moms just shouldn't *have* birthdays," Joe said without looking up from his work. Parents in general, he added silently. "They've been around so long, they've gotten every possible present."

"Nice," said Nick. "Make sure you write that on the card." He shook his head hopelessly, then turned to a page in one magazine that made him stop and smile. "Hey, here's something," he announced. "'Top Five Things Moms Want Most for Their Birthday.'"

"Excellent!" Kevin cried. He and Joe jumped up and joined Nick.

"Number five is a candle that smells like spaghetti," Nick reported.

Joe shook his head. "She's got one," he reminded them. "And she's never even lit it," he added, looking offended.

"Number four, a gold monkey clock that

howls on the hour," Nick said.

Joe shook his head again. He reached over to a shelf and pulled down a gold monkey clock just like the one in the magazine picture. "Two birthdays ago," he said. The clock suddenly howled. "Still running fast."

"Okay," Nick went on, "this is weird. Number three is dinner with Joe." He turned to his brother, who looked equally shocked by this bit of news.

"I'm number *three*?" Joe complained. "What's number two?"

Nick turned back to the magazine. "A vacation with the family."

"And number one?" Joe asked.

This was getting odder by the moment. What kind of magazine was Nick reading?

"A vacation *without* the family," said Nick.

The boys had to laugh. That actually made sense.

Then suddenly, they looked up to see their parents walking in. Their dad, Tom Lucas, was carrying a crate; their mom, Sandy, a humongous smile.

As his dad set down his crate, Nick quickly shoved aside the various magazines.

"What are you hiding?" Mrs. Lucas asked, her "mom sense" instantly going on the alert as she took in the boys' guilty expressions.

Nick smiled as innocently as possible. Maybe if he didn't say anything, they would drop it. But no such luck.

"*Nick.*" His father frowned.

Nick sighed, then he showed them the collection of magazines.

"*Women's* magazines?" his dad said when he saw them.

"We're uh"—Nick tried to think—"doing research on . . ."

"Women," Joe spoke up.

Kevin nodded. "For a new song about . . ."

"Women," Joe repeated.

Their dad didn't look convinced. Neither did their mom, for that matter.

"We want to write it as . . ." Nick began to add.

"Women," Joe said—again.

Nick looked at him. "He means from a female perspective," he explained to their mom and dad. He was dying to change the subject. He pointed to the plastic crate. "So, whatcha got *there*?" he asked.

The distraction worked. "Your dad found the old home movies I thought we lost during the move," Mrs. Lucas replied, picking up the crate. She pulled out an old VHS cassette to show them.

Exciting, the boys thought—*not!* Who still had VHS tapes? Hadn't they gone the way of the dinosaurs?

Joe stepped up beside her. "Hey, Mom," he said, trying to sound extracasual, "of course, we've already gotten your birthday present. But just out of curiosity, what do you want for your birthday?"

All three boys held their breath and waited for her to answer.

"Honey," Mrs. Lucas said, "I have everything I want." She let the words sink in and gave them a big smile. "As long as my family is safe, healthy, and together."

CHAPTER THREE

"**W**hy does she have to make it so hard?" Nick muttered to Kevin a moment later as their mom took the VHS tape and crossed over to their flat-screen TV. Apparently, the *Lucases* still had a VHS player.

"What are *you* getting Mom?" Joe whispered to their dad.

"Well"—his dad grinned—"last year I really nailed it."

Surprised, the boys shared an "Oh, really?" look. They remembered the entire JONAS wardrobe—T-shirt, cap, and scarf—plus whirly light and poster that their dad had given their mom. Nailed it? Not so much.

"How am I going to top that, right?" Mr. Lucas went on. "Then it hit me," he told them, growing more excited, "island birthday party! I'm going to rent an island, preferably volcanic—"

But their mom overheard him. "No more shmancy parties!" she called from across the room. Silently she added, I'm still recovering from Presidents Day on a jumbo jet. Of all the members of the Lucas family, she missed their old, regular life the most. "I just want a little get-together, like a *normal* family," she said.

She gave them all a meaningful look, then turned back to the television. The tape she'd slipped in was already playing. "Awww, look how cute you boys were! Come watch," she called.

Mr. Lucas shrugged and walked over, but Nick

held Joe and Kevin back. "I just got a great idea for Mom's present," he said.

Kevin grinned and nodded. "I think we're thinking the same thing, bro."

"Transfer all those old home movies onto DVD!" Nick cried, reaching out to shake his hand.

But Kevin kept his hand down as his face turned from eager to confused. "*And* get her an otter that can play the trumpet?" he asked.

Nick shook his head. "No," he said. "Just the DVDs."

Kevin slapped his forehead. "We weren't thinking the same thing *at all*, bro," he said.

Nick rolled his eyes at Kevin, then turned to his other brother. They had to get a plan in order. "We can re-edit the home movies and play them for everyone at her birthday party." He didn't say it out loud because he was always getting picked on for being too sensitive, but he couldn't help but think how cool it would be to make their family history high quality.

"That's awesome!" Joe exclaimed. "Plus, on DVD, they'll never get ruined."

"Sweetie!" their mom called to one of them from the sofa. "Come see this! You were the cutest child in the world."

Psyched about their plan (though not too wild about watching boring old home movies), the boys joined their parents. They were in for a quite a surprise.

Ew! was all they could think as they viewed their long-forgotten, younger selves. Their home movies weren't boring—they were humiliating.

On the screen, a two-year old Nick sat in front of a birthday cake.

"Smile for the camera," Mr. Lucas said from behind the lens.

Toddler Nick remained stone-faced. Even when his mom asked, he didn't move a muscle on his face.

Watching the video, Kevin laughed. "Nick didn't smile until he was what, four?" he asked.

Nick turned and frowned. "I wanted to wait

until I had all my teeth," he explained.

"Hey," said their dad as the tape skipped ahead, "look! Our first Christmas in the firehouse."

"Remember, Grandma burned those cookies, and we had to call the fire department?" Joe said, reminiscing.

"And our own phone rang," Nick added.

They all laughed.

"Man, time goes by fast," Mr. Lucas said. He put his arm around his wife.

"Yes, it does," she agreed. Then she sniffed . . . or was that Joe?

Nick turned to his brother. "Are you crying?" he asked Joe.

"What?" Joe looked away. "Me? No. A bug just flew into my eye." He sniffed again and pretended to bat it away. Then he turned to Kevin. "Are *you* crying?"

Kevin's lip trembled, then a sob spilled out. "Yes!"

His mom reached out to smooth his hair. "It's

okay," she said gently, "this stuff is emotional." She leaned against her husband and looked up into his eyes. "I can't tell you how much I love these movies, honey," she said. Then her own sentimental tears began to pour out, too.

"You okay?" Joe asked.

Mrs. Lucas heaved a sob-filled sigh and nodded.

"She's not sad crying, she's happy crying," Joe's dad assured him. He glanced at his wife, just to be sure, and she nodded again . . . and cried more.

Just then, Stella Malone walked in, along with the youngest Lucas, Frankie.

"Hey, all," announced Stella cheerfully. "I wanted to run these designs by—" She suddenly noticed the video playing on the TV. "Aww, home movies," she said, grinning. Then she noticed Mrs. Lucas weeping. "Happy crying?" she asked, checking.

The boys' mom nodded once again. Then, finding a tissue, she blew her nose.

"Where's *me*?" Frankie asked, moving closer to the TV.

"These are from before you were born," his dad explained.

Frankie frowned and turned dismissively away from the screen. Where was the fun in that? he wondered. It was bad enough, being the only Lucas brother *not* in the JONAS band. Did he have to be left out of old home movies, too?

He waved to his family as he strolled out of the room. "Frankie, out," he said.

Stella, meanwhile, was watching the big screen, enthralled. "Is that Joe?!" She gasped. "What's his hair doing? It's got a sort of swirl thing happening."

Nick nodded and chuckled. "Like the top of a frozen yogurt," he agreed.

Joe reached for the remote. "I think we've seen enough," he said.

But Kevin snatched it away. "Oh, no, we haven't!" He grinned. It was always fun to see his brother looking less rock star and more, well, dork.

"Look at that adorable little girl!" Stella suddenly exclaimed. "Look at those eyes. And that hair! Look at that smile. Is that the cutest smile you've ever seen?"

Joe looked at the screen more closely. "Stella, that's you," he said.

"I know!" She took the remote from Kevin's hand and plopped down on the sofa. Then, she happily turned up the volume. Forget about going over the JONAS wardrobe, she thought. She could watch her younger, equally adorable self all day!

CHAPTER FOUR

While Joe waited impatiently for Stella to tire of watching herself in old home movies, Nick and Kevin went ahead and got busy making birthday plans for their mom.

At last, Joe convinced Stella that she really had to go. She still had to wrap the scarf for their mom, didn't she? Then he collected all the tapes, returned them to the plastic crate, and carried them into the kitchen just as Kevin walked through the back door with a bulging bag of groceries.

"Where do you want me to keep these tapes?" Joe asked him.

"Anywhere, I guess," Kevin answered with a shrug. "Nick's going to find a place to transfer them to DVD."

Joe set the crate down on the floor next to the kitchen counter, then looked more closely at the bag Kevin had just put down. "Whatcha got there?" he asked.

"It's a little extra present for Mom," Kevin explained. He pulled out a carton of eggs, a box of cake mix, and a can of frosting. He arranged them neatly together. "A do-it-yourself birthday cake!" he exclaimed.

"Very classy," Joe said. What kind of gift was that for their mom? She cooked and baked enough as it was. "How about *we* make the cake *for* her?" he suggested.

Kevin considered the idea. "But we don't know how to bake a cake," he pointed out correctly.

As if on cue, Nick slid down the fire pole wearing a chef's apron and a tall white hat. "I'm not an expert," he began, "but I made a few dozen cupcakes when I was five, and I got that second-place ribbon for my banana bread when I was eleven, and let's not forget my Floating Coconut Flambé."

Slowly, Joe and Kevin began to smile. Oh, right! How could they have forgotten their little brother's secret talent? Nick was practically a certified pastry chef! Birthday-cake baking? Bring it on!

Nick tightened his apron. "Gentlemen," he declared, "let's bake a cake."

Before long, all three brothers were covered with flour—and so was the Lucas kitchen. Every cabinet was open. Pots and pans were scattered over the counters and the floor. And they'd barely begun!

"Okay," said Nick, "we're ready to get started." He first looked at Joe. "You get a bowl." Then he turned to face Kevin. "You pour the batter," he announced.

Joe beamed as he searched the crowded counters for a bowl. They had to mix in one more ingredient before they could pour the batter into the cake pans. "We are *rockin'* Mom's birthday!" he declared.

Nick handed the almost finished batter to Kevin.

"Batter up!" Kevin said.

Joe held out the bowl he'd found for Kevin. "Hey, batter, batter, batter!" he joked. He watched as Kevin poured it in. "More batter!" he called.

Happily, Kevin poured more . . . and more . . . and more into the bowl. "Weird," he said.

He and Joe looked down at the bowl which just didn't seem to fill, no matter how much batter they poured in.

"It's like a mysterious bottomless bowl," Joe observed.

Nick spun around. "Mysterious bowl"? That

sounded suspicious. He looked over at Joe's bowl which now wasn't just not full—it was nearly empty.

"Dudes, that's not a bowl," he cried. "That's a colander!"

Joe and Kevin looked at each other. "What's a colander?" they both asked.

Nick slapped his forehead with his hand, leaving a long flour smudge across his face. "Something only you guys would call a 'mysterious bottomless bowl.'" He groaned. "A colander has holes in the bottom."

Joe held up the bowl and examined the bottom. Yep. Sure enough. Full of holes. Then he glanced down to see where all the batter had gone to. . . . Yep. Sure enough. All over the crate of videos!

Joe slowly set down the colander, and with a full-of-holes feeling in his stomach, reached down and picked up the crate and set it down in front of his brothers. Every inch of every tape was completely covered in sticky goo.

"We need towels!" Kevin cried.

They raced around the kitchen. Where did their mom keep her towels again?

To make matters worse, at that moment, their dad came into the kitchen.

"What's that smell?" Mr. Lucas asked, sniffing the air.

They all turned to the box of tapes, which was smoking. Joe had set the crate down on top of the stove—and it was turned on!

Nick lunged to turn off the stove, while Kevin found the fire extinguisher and started to blast away. Soon the stove was covered with batter, melted videos, and foam.

"Tell me that's not what I think it is," Mr. Lucas said, his face growing pale.

Horrified, Joe fished out one of the smoking, dripping cassettes and held it up. "All our home movies," he said with a moan.

"We killed them," wailed Nick.

Kevin choked back a sob.

Then a voice none of them wanted to hear

spoke up. "What is going on here?!"

The boys spun around, eyes wide and mouths open, to see their mother standing by the back door. Her face was ashen, and her hands were shaking. Frankie stood beside her, calmly eating an ice-cream cone.

"Are those . . . our family movies?" She choked.

"Mom—" Nick began. Then he stopped. What was there, really, to say? Besides, by then their mom was bawling and wouldn't have heard him anyway.

"I don't think that's happy crying," Kevin said with a gulp.

As the brothers stood there helplessly, their mom ran past them, out of the kitchen. They could hear her sobs all the way to her room.

Ashamed, their eyes moved from the videos to the floor, then, miserably, to one another. It was safe to say that *never* had they felt so utterly awful before.

Frankie, who was still there, stared at them

sternly. "We are very disappointed in you boys,"
he said. Then he, too, walked past, taking one
last lick of ice cream before adding his half-eaten
cone to the crate full of goo.

CHAPTER FIVE

Nick, Kevin, and Joe worked hard to clean up the kitchen as best they could. And by the time they were done, it was pretty near spotless. Still, it didn't make them feel any better as they sat down at the dinner table that night.

The table was quiet and uncomfortable as the three brothers pushed their food around their plates. None of them had much of an appetite.

Suddenly, an alarm beeped. Mr. Lucas looked

at his watch and then at his sons.

"All right boys," he said. "It's been five minutes. Apologize to your mother again."

Nick was the first to speak. "Mom . . . we really feel horrible about this."

"I know you do," their mom said.

"We are so sorry," Kevin told her.

"I know you are," she answered.

"Apparently, a colander is some kind of bowl with holes in it," Joe confessed.

Mrs. Lucas nodded. "I know it is. And I want you to know that I love you more than anything in the world." Then, sadly but still sweetly, she got up and left the kitchen.

No! the boys thought. *No!*

Nick groaned. "Why does she have to make it so *hard*?" he wailed.

The only thing worse than breaking your mother's heart had to be having her forgive you for it! They'd be much happier, they knew, if she grounded them for life. Or eternity even. That they could handle. That they deserved. But having her tell them that it was okay, that she loved them anyway—they'd never be able to take it.

Later that night, the boys were in their room, hiding. Joe shook his head. "We batter, burn, and foam all her memories, and she forgives us." He squeezed his eyes shut and shook his fists.

Nick nodded sadly. "And she'll never mention it again, and she'll be totally sweet and loving—"

"It's going to be torture!" Joe cried.

They writhed about, as if in pain, imagining the lifetime of guilt and misery ahead. Suddenly, Kevin sat up in his bed. "Wait a minute!" he said. "I've got an idea! We can't save the tapes, but we *can* save the memories."

Joe glanced at him, curious. "Kevin, it sounds like you have a scheme in mind and we're supposed to ask you what it is."

He and Nick waited.

"Oh, right!" said Kevin. "Me!" He nodded excitedly. "We get a camera, build sets, ask Stella to help with costumes, then reenact our home movies and videotape them." He looked from Joe to Nick, eager for his brothers' reaction.

Nick sighed. Remake years and years—and hours and hours—worth of family history? Well, okay. Why not?

"And I was worried it was going to be something ridiculous." Nick grinned.

CHAPTER SIX

The boys got right to work, and in less than an hour they were ready for the first segment: Halloween circa 1992.

Joe wore a cowboy costume, Kevin was Abe Lincoln, and Nick, who was dressed as a tiger, had landed the job of filming. A safe position, as it was turning out.

"Action!" Nick cried.

Joe and Kevin stepped up to the firehouse's

front door, holding empty plastic pumpkin baskets in their hands. "Trick or . . . Trick or . . ." Joe began. Thoughtfully, he touched his finger to his chin.

"*Treat!*" Nick called out. "Trick or *treat!*"

But Joe turned to him and shook his head. "Everyone says 'trick or treat,'" he said. "I'm trying to take the character in a whole new direction."

Nick rolled his eyes. "You're a Halloween cowboy!" he replied impatiently. "There are no other directions to take it in."

Joe thought for a moment. "What about a zombie cowboy?" he suggested. He grinned. "A zombie cowboy might say . . ." He made his eyes big and creepy and held out his arms. "'Trick or braaaains!'" Then he laughed.

"I can't work under these conditions." Nick groaned. He turned off the camera and angrily stomped away.

Next came Christmas. Nick, Kevin, and Joe

were all dressed in footed pajamas—a look that was rather hard to pull off as teenagers. This time it was Joe's turn to record.

"Lights!" he yelled.

Nick gave a thumbs-up, then plugged in the lights on a small plastic Christmas tree.

"Snow!" hollered Joe.

From the top of a ladder, Kevin caught Joe's signal. He nodded and began to toss handfuls of foam packing peanuts.

"Stella!" Joe cried next.

Reluctantly, Stella Malone walked in front of the camera in her own footed pajamas, with an enormous set of orthodontic headgear wrapped around her head.

"Okay, everybody," Joe directed, "grab your eggnog!"

Bitterly, Stella turned toward him. "I'm not doing this," she muttered through her muzzle of headgear. "We all know what's going to happen. I drink the eggnog, my headgear makes it spill down the front of me, and I get a rash on

Christmas." Of all the scenes they had to reenact, she thought, did they really have to include this one?

Nick looked up at her beseechingly from his place beside the Christmas tree. "This is one of our mom's most cherished memories," he told her.

Stella looked from Nick to Joe to Kevin, who were all silently begging her, and sighed. "Roll 'em," she said through gritted, metal-clad teeth.

Joe grinned and restarted the camera, and they all raised their glasses of eggnog. Then they drank . . . and to everyone's surprise, Stella was fine. No drips. No spills. No Christmas rash. Stella smiled.

"Cut," Joe said. "Stella, what are you doing?"

Stella shrugged. "My mouth is bigger now." Her smile widened. "I'm sorry," she said insincerely.

Kevin shook his head. This wouldn't do. "Why do you hate our mom?" he asked.

Stella's smile faded, and her shoulders slumped. She poured herself another cup of eggnog. Of course she didn't hate their mom!

"Roll 'em," she said again.

Once more, the cast raised their glasses. "Merry Christmas!" They all toasted.

The boys drank, watching Stella as they did. But instead of raising her cup all the way to her caged lips, Stella simply dumped the eggnog out onto her chest. "Happy?" she said.

The brothers grinned and clapped. They were *very* happy, it seemed.

So far the brothers had to admit that re-creating their family's old home movies had gone even better than planned.

"Okay," Kevin said, leading his brothers down the fire pole for their next nostalgic scene, "when Nick blows out the candles on his second birthday cake, I think we should set up over—" All of a sudden he spotted his headless tripod and stopped. "Where's the camcorder?" he blurted out.

He turned to Nick. *He* hadn't moved it. Then Nick turned to Joe. "Joe?" he said.

Joe held up his hands. "I didn't touch it," he told them.

"It has everything we shot on it!" Kevin declared.

Nick and Joe looked at each other in total panic. They *had* to find that camera. They instantly split up to look.

They searched all over the kitchen . . . the living room . . . their loft . . . and while they found plenty of *other* cameras—disposable cameras, underwater cameras, digital cameras, Polaroid cameras, Super 8 cameras, pocket-size cameras, suitcase-size cameras, even some that were antique—*their* camera was nowhere—*nowhere*—to be found!

When there were no more crevices, nooks, crannies, hidey holes, or closets left, they regrouped in a state of hysteria and shock.

"We ruin the original home movies and then lose the new ones! We're amazing!" Nick cried. This truly was turning into the biggest birthday disaster of all time.

All that hard work for nothing! All that guilt that they'd now never lose!

Maybe there was still some place they hadn't looked, some small, secret, hidden, obscure hole in the wall. Nick tugged at his curly hair, Joe closed his eyes, and Kevin looked—well, like Kevin. Each one racked his brain, until all of a sudden, Frankie came strolling through the back door. He stopped and stood in the doorway, smirking.

He was smirking *too* much. His brothers turned on him instantly, eyes steely and narrowed. Of course! They should have known.

"Where is it, Frankie?" Kevin said.

"Where's what?" Frankie replied innocently.

"The video camera," Joe stated coldly.

Frankie looked thoughtful. He scratched his wavy-haired head. "Silver and black?" he asked. He held his up hands, a few inches apart. "About this big?"

"That's the one," Joe said.

Frankie nodded and rubbed his chin. He

wasn't going to offer up anything else.

Kevin huffed and got out his wallet. Enough already, he thought. Good-old Frankie, always getting one up on us. Kevin opened the bill pocket and counted. "Okay, I've got about seventeen dollars." He turned to Nick and Joe. "What about you guys?"

They reached into their own pockets, but Frankie shook his head. "Uh-uh," he said. "I don't want the money."

Not about money? Joe, Nick, and Kevin stared at him. Then what?

"I want to be in the movies," Frankie said simply.

Joe held up his hands. "But you weren't born yet, Frankie," he replied.

Frankie shrugged. "I'm born now."

His three older brothers looked at each other. Then they shrugged, too. Why not?

CHAPTER SEVEN

It only took a second for Frankie to get the camera from its hiding place under his bed (the one place none of them had dared look—you never knew what you might find there). Then *all* the boys got right to work finishing their movie for their mom. After all, as well as Thanksgiving dinner, they still had three more birthdays, two school plays, a day at the zoo, and a major-league baseball game to re-create—all before their mother's *normal-family* birthday party was set to begin.

At long last, they were done. They strung some streamers around the living room and went to get their mom.

"What's going on?" she asked as they took her by the arms and led her gently to the sofa.

"We know how upset you are about the home movies," Joe began.

"I'm not upset," their mom insisted with a tight smile.

Their dad nodded in agreement as he joined her on the couch. "Boys, your mom is not upset," he told them. But when she wasn't looking, he gave them a clear "Oh, yes, she is!" look.

Nick couldn't take it any longer. "You're killing us with kindness, Mom!" he declared.

Their mother sighed and looked at each of them. "All right," she admitted, "I'm upset."

Nick, Kevin, and Joe clasped their hands, relieved. "Thank you!" they said.

"But what good does it do to take it out on

my boys?" Mrs. Lucas asked them. She looked away rather painfully. "You didn't *mean* to cut out a mother's heart."

Ooh. Yeah. That one hurt. Maybe being killed with kindness actually *was* better than the truth, Nick thought.

But then Kevin took her hand. "We realize we can never replace the home movies that Joe ruined," he began.

Joe turned to him. "Me?! *You* poured the batter!" he shouted.

"*You* got the bowl with the holes in it!" Kevin shot back.

"It's a *colander*!" Joe cried.

Mrs. Lucas held up her hands to shush them. "Guys, guys," she said. She'd had enough of the bickering already. They must have brought her here for some reason. "What's this all about?" she asked.

Nick hit PLAY on the remote he was holding. "We redid the home movies, Mom," he said as the screen came to life.

A handwritten card appeared on the TV's big screen. THE HOME MOVIES PART TWO, it read.

Mrs. Lucas gasped as up on the screen, Joe and Kevin appeared in their Halloween costumes. Mrs. Lucas couldn't believe her eyes. And neither could she believe the Christmases, school plays, or Thanksgivings that followed.

"I can't believe you did this," she said softly, a hand to her heart.

Then Frankie grabbed her arm and pointed to the screen. "Here comes the best part!" he said.

They all turned back to the TV to see Kevin, Joe, and Nick (in a large, teddy-bear–covered bib), seated around the kitchen table, with Stella dressed as Mrs. Lucas, and Frankie, in a suit and tie just like his dad's, "carving" a big plastic turkey.

Their dad immediately started to laugh. His wife, on the other hand, grabbed his arm and started to cry.

"Uh-oh," Kevin said.

"Sad crying?" Joe said gently, almost afraid to ask.

But Mrs. Lucas sniffled and emphatically shook her head no.

"Happy crying?" Nick asked hopefully.

But again, their mom shook her head no.

Their dad grinned. "Proud crying?"

At last their mom nodded. Then she wiped her eyes. "This is the best birthday present I've ever gotten," she said. "And you know what? I think I like the new home movies even better than the old ones," she said. Then she scrunched up her face and began to cry all over again. She was going to have to reapply her makeup before the party.

Joe, Nick, and Kevin pumped their fists in the air. "Yes!" they cheered. Those words sounded better than a stadium full of screaming fans.

Still smiling, the family watched as the scene shifted, and the screen was suddenly filled with bodies just seen from the waist down.

"What's this?" Mrs. Lucas asked, puzzled. She

tried to think but couldn't remember any home movies quite like that.

Nick grinned and rubbed his youngest brother's head. "Frankie wanted to direct," he explained.

The party, suffice it to say, was a huge success. The *new* "old home movies" were a hit. And when Stella saw how happy they made Mrs. Lucas, she realized that even reliving a Christmas rash was worth it. Not that she would ever tell the boys that, of course.

"I have to admit," Stella told Mrs. Lucas, "those turned out pretty good."

Unfortunately, Kevin overheard the comment. He grabbed the remote. The show wasn't over quite yet. "Hold on," he told everybody. "We have to watch the special features."

Stella felt a warning tingle in her stomach. Why was Kevin looking at her as he said "special"?

On the screen, a young girl with blond hair stood talking to someone off-camera. The girl was dressed in a long black dress. Watching, Stella smiled. It was her!

The young Stella was wearing one of her mother's gowns. "I love that dress," the older Stella said to Mrs. Lucas. "Too bad it doesn't fit me now."

The Stella on screen had stuffed two balloons in the top. Apparently it hadn't fit then, either.

"Too small?" Mrs. Lucas asked now.

"Too big," Stella answered. Behind her, Joe chuckled. "*That's* for sure."

Stella's shoulders went up. Joe gulped. Uh-oh. Slowly, she turned to face him. "Oh, no you just didn't," she snarled.

Joe sniffed dramatically. "Something else is burning in the kitchen," he observed. "I better check it out." And then he took off.

"You *better* run!" called Stella, jumping up to chase him.

But Mrs. Lucas just sat, smiling, gazing at the screen. Footsteps thundered from above, while the constant screams of adoring fans drifted in from outside. Still, Mrs. Lucas couldn't have asked for a better birthday. Some people might say it wasn't exactly "normal," sure. But by now she'd come to realize that it was about as close as she could get. And to tell the truth, that was just fine with her. She wouldn't have traded being the mother of the JONAS band for anything in the world.

Don't miss a beat! Check out another book in the JONAS series.

ᴄDOUBLE TAKE

Adapted by Marianne Schaberg

Based on the series created by Michael Curtis & Roger S. H. Schulman

Based on the episode, "That Ding You Do," Written by Heather MacGillvray & Linda Mathious

It was just a typical afternoon in the Lucas household. Kevin, Nick, and Joe were lounging in their living room. Their living room, however, *wasn't* so typical.

The boys lived in a converted firehouse with their parents and younger brother, Frankie. Sliding down a pole when breakfast was ready wasn't the only thing that set the three Lucas brothers apart from other teenagers—they also happened to be mega rock stars. They were so famous that their pictures were plastered on the walls of teenage girls' rooms everywhere. Together, the brothers made up the hottest rock band on the planet, JONAS.

That afternoon, Kevin, the oldest member of JONAS, was working on his pecs, lifting twenty-pound weights in the corner. He needed to stay fit if he was going to jam out practically every night onstage. Nick sat on a stool strumming his guitar, practicing a new song for the band. Sprawled out on the couch, Joe wasn't working quite so hard; he was reading *Teenster Magazine*.

"Hey, guys, there's a new 'How well do you know JONAS?' quiz in here!" Joe called out, flipping to a page in the magazine. He was eager to test his knowledge of his brothers and best buds. "Let's see how well I know . . . Joe!"

Joe went through each question aloud: "'Yes . . . No . . . Armadillo . . . No . . . Yes.'"

Holding up the magazine, Joe jumped up on

the couch. "All right! Five out of five! I'm a . . ." He searched for his score. "'Real Joe nut,'" he read.

Curious, Kevin and Nick walked over to check out the quiz. Reading over Joe's shoulder Nick raised an eyebrow. "Hey, your favorite snack isn't cherry pudding," he said to Kevin.

Kevin shook his head. "It's chocolate tacos. And your favorite color isn't medium spring green. It's electric indigo," he told Nick as he flopped down on the couch, dejected.

Pulling the magazine away from Joe, Kevin read his profile. Everything was wrong! This meant war! "We need to straighten out *Teenster Magazine*!" he cried.

Excited by the prospect of putting the magazine in its place, Kevin turned to his brothers and went on. "We should write a letter to the editor," he said and searched for the editor's name in the magazine.

Joe was as eager as his brothers to prove a point to the magazine—even if they had gotten some of *his* favorites right. "Who's got a pen?" he asked.

Fumbling through his pockets, Nick shook his head. No luck. Kevin shrugged. He didn't have a pen either. Within seconds, Joe had a solution; he jumped up and ran over to one of the windows in the living room.

As soon as he opened the window, the sound of hundreds of screaming girls poured into the firehouse. On a daily basis, girls surrounded the Lucas home, patiently waiting for just one peek at the band. This caused a serious problem for the boys and their family. They couldn't even buy groceries without getting swarmed. But it could also help in certain situations.

Bracing himself, Joe peeked his head out the window. The screams rose to a deafening roar. Putting his hands up to his mouth, Joe shouted, "Excuse me, girls! Anyone got a pen?"

As soon as the words left his mouth, a blizzard of pens came flying through the window. Joe ducked. Turning around, he saw the pens sticking out of the wall in a perfect heart-shaped pattern. Those girls had some pretty good aim. Joe stood up and yelled out to them, "Thank you!"

Shutting the window, he walked over to the pens, pulled one out of the wall and sat down with his brothers to write a strongly worded letter to the editor.